i

LYCAON

THE STORY OF THE FIRST WEREWOLF

WRITTEN BY

BRENDAN SCHWEDA

ILLUSTRATED BY

LIZ EMIRZIAN

EDITED BY

SARAH ZAR

A. KECK PRESS

New York

Printed in the United States of America

First Printing, 2013

ISBN 978-0-9910466-0-7

A. Keck Press
New York, New York

www.BTSchweda.com

www.LizEmirzian.com

Special Thanks

From the author:

Thanks to my family, and to the following individuals, for their support:

Jon Earle, Ron Tereshyn, Andrew Schweda,
George H. Buddin, Jeffrey Miller,
Ben & Carly Kinberg,
Larsen & Stephanie Eisenberg,
John Druzba, Adam Redmer,
Paul & Erin Morie, Trey Jarrell, Zach Goodwin,
Robert Rice, and Tim O'Leary

From the illustrator:

Special thanks to my mother Carole Barrett,
who has always supported and encouraged me
without hesitation. Also to my father, Paul Emirzian,
whose wild heart and artistic creativeness was
passed down to me and will remain with me
for all my life.

Lycaon:
the Story of the First Werewolf

This book is dedicated to
Neil and Helen Schweda,
who taught me how to love stories.

INTRODUCTION

In Greek mythology, there is a brief story about an unfortunate encounter between Zeus and King Lycaon, of Arcadia. The meeting ends with Zeus enraged, and Lycaon cursed to become the first werewolf of Western tradition. That myth does not include one of the fundamental characters of time-tested werewolf lore; namely, the moon. After digging through multiple works by ancient Greek writers, I unearthed the possibility for a much more complex, and perhaps quietly guarded, story. Bits and pieces of existing myths were fashioned together for this telling. So, if you recognize portions of what you read, it is no accident. The rest of the story was fleshed out with my own speculation about details that may have been altered or left unsaid through the years.

This story has existed in bits and pieces for hundreds of years, but this is the first time that it's been recorded in its entirety.

It is the story of the first werewolf. However, it is also the story of a king, a goddess, a god, and a child.

The story begins in Arcadia, an ancient and legendary Greek city. The first king of Arcadia was Lycaon. King Lycaon was a righteous and respected ruler who built up Arcadia from nothing to greatness.

One day, Lycaon set out early in the morning to hunt. After a full day of hunting, the king returned home with plenty of game, filled his belly, and fell asleep content in his bed.

In the middle of the night, the king stirred and his eyes opened. He found himself at the edge of a wood and spied his palace in the distance. Lycaon observed that while there were no lights in the sky, he could clearly identify his surroundings.

The king turned to see a lone brilliant light emanating from deep within the woods. The light drew closer and brighter while the king stood steadfast to discover the source.

When the light was almost upon the king, it took the form of a woman. She was the most beautiful woman that Lycaon had ever seen. However, she shone so brightly that the king could only glimpse her face.

Her presence was more of an impression or a feeling, rather than the details of her eyes, nose, or a mouth. The lady leaned forward and kissed Lycaon upon the head. The king immediately woke in his bed.

Lycaon did not leave his bedroom for three straight days. He tried with all of his might to remain in the blissful moment of the faceless lady's kiss. The king had no idea who the woman was, but he was determined to find out.

For the next nine nights, the king went out in search of the lady. He snuck out of his palace while everyone slept, and waited for her at the edge of the wood.

As each night passed, the light of the moon shone brighter than the night before. It occurred to the king on the ninth night, when the moon was fullest, that the light shining down on him was the same as the light that had shone from the wood. The king realized, then, that the lady from the wood must be no other than the great huntress and moon goddess, Artemis.

Once, when Artemis was only three years old, she sat upon her father Zeus's knee. The god asked his daughter what kind of gifts she would like. The first three things the child asked for were: eternal virginity, as many names as her brother Apollo, and a silver bow with silver arrows. The god granted his daughter all of these things and more.

As Lycaon considered what a powerful and respected goddess had come to visit him, his desire to see her increased. The king erected a temple at the edge of the wood where the goddess had appeared. For the next nine months, on the night of each full moon, Lycaon worshiped Artemis in the temple and made a sacrifice to her. He begged the goddess to visit him again.

While he was in the temple on the night of the ninth month, the king fell asleep. Lycaon found himself, again, in the mist of a dream. Although his eyes were open, the king could not move. Abruptly, Artemis appeared before him in all of her glory. She reclined with the king and allowed him to worship her completely.

In the morning, the king and the goddess each returned to their usual duties. Not long after their intimate encounter, Artemis went to bathe one afternoon in a small pool. She disrobed herself and noticed a small bump about her naked belly. The goddess had become pregnant.

Artemis immediately transformed herself into a bear and retreated deep into the woods. She preferred to be killed by wild beasts or hunters, rather than face her father and tell him that she had betrayed his gift of virginity.

While she lay in hiding, Artemis's own hunting dogs caught on to her scent. The dogs did not recognize her in the form of a bear. As the dogs were about to attack, Zeus scooped up Artemis and her unborn child to safety. The child was delivered and he was called Arcas.

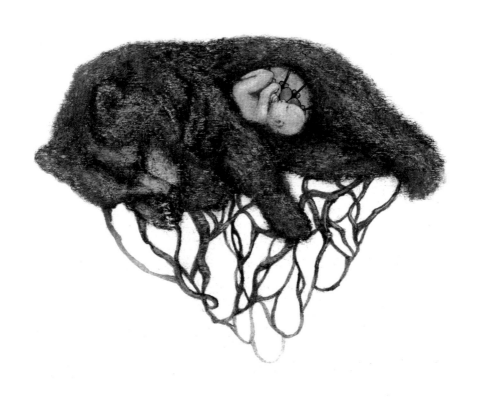

Zeus did not punish Artemis for breaking her virginal bond, nor did he punish her child. Zeus did not ask who the baby's father was. The god requested only that Artemis preserve her chaste reputation and bestow the infant to someone else's care. Artemis obeyed her father's wish and entrusted the child to Lycaon in secret.

Boys were not unusual in Lycaon's household. The king had many wives, and by them, many sons. Some say that the sons numbered as many as fifty. They were impious and mischievous young men who often incurred the anger of the gods.

One day, not long after Arcas entered Lycaon's household, an old man came to the palace door and asked for a night's food and lodging. Lycaon graciously abided. However, Lycaon's sons were not so hospitable. They found the stranger to be suspicious. They began to chide him and demanded to know his business.

The man revealed himself as Zeus in the flesh. The god declared that he had come to administer punishment for impiety. Lycaon decided that Zeus had come to punish him for his affair with Artemis. In a panic, Lycaon scooped up the sleeping babe Arcas from his cradle, and lay the child down at Zeus's feet. The king begged for forgiveness, declared that he would erase his mistake, and slit the child's throat.

Zeus had no idea who the child's father was until that moment. The god had come only to punish Lycaon's impious sons. Zeus looked down at the limp body of his dead grandchild and then looked to Lycaon with scorn.

In an instant, Lycaon found himself back at the edge of the wood. He spied his palace far in the distance and it was crumbling in flames. The king arched his back and screamed toward the sky in despair.

His cry was not the cry of a man, but rather the howl of a beast. Lycaon looked down as drool fell from his mouth. It landed next to gnarly paws instead of hands. The king had been transformed into a wolf.

Zeus had destroyed the household and cast out the king. Some say that Zeus killed all of the king's sons in that moment. Others say that the sons were cast out and turned into wolves as well.

Lycaon could not return to his people. Those who lived in the villages surrounding the palace, now in shambles, did not like wolves. Wolves were dangerous to both livestock and children. If the king ran to his people for sanctuary, he would surely be killed.

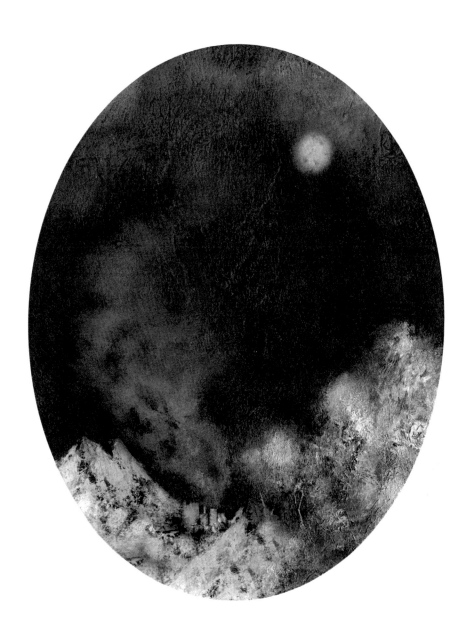

The wolf-king decided to retreat into the wood. It was his only refuge. Lycaon had hunted in that forest for years. He knew where both the dangerous beasts and easy prey resided. The king set forth deep into the wood with faith in his ability to survive.

Over time, the king learned to live as a beast. Thoughts of his kingdom and people faded into memory. Finally, in the ninth year of Lycaon's exile, Artemis approached her father. The goddess begged Zeus to restore the king to his human form. Zeus agreed to restore Lycaon, and allowed him to return to his people, on one condition. On the night of each full moon, when Artemis was her brightest and able to visit with the king, Lycaon would be transformed back into the shape of a wolf.

Lycaon did not know that his return to humanity was conditional. The king knew only that after nine long years of living wild, he was restored to the form of a man while drinking from a stream. He returned to find his palace rebuilt and was welcomed by his people. Lycaon sang praises to Artemis. He had decided that only the goddess could have convinced Zeus to undo the curse.

On the night of the next full moon, Lycaon worshiped Artemis in the temple at the edge of the wood. The king smiled in the moonlight and thanked the goddess for rescuing him after nine arduous years. No sooner did the moonlight cover the king's face than his body crumbled into a wolfen shape. Lycaon howled in torment and ran toward his palace. He refused to be isolated in the woods again.

The king arrived at the edge of a village outside the palace. He came upon a young girl, who was alone on the road and fetching water for her family. The full moon shone down on the girl's features and blurred them so that Lycaon saw only Artemis standing before him. In that moment, the wolf-king was both man and beast. The king was elated to see his lover again. However, the wolf saw only the individual who must have betrayed him back into bondage.

Lycaon ran toward the girl, who stood frozen before him. He lunged at her with outstretched arms and tore her to pieces. The king looked down at his bloody body and then howled at the moon in agony. He cursed the name of Artemis for what he had become.

Zeus approached Artemis after he observed what Lycaon had done. The god told his daughter that she had a decision to make. Either she must kill the king, or Zeus would do it himself. The goddess chose to kill Lycaon herself. She killed him swiftly and mercifully with her painless silver arrows. These are the same silver arrows that Zeus had bestowed to his daughter when she was a child. They are also the same arrows which Artemis once used to slay the hunter, Orion.

With Lycaon dead, who would tell the king's story? Artemis would not betray her own virginal reputation and Zeus would certainly not blemish his daughter's name. There are those who say that we may have Lycaon's many sons to thank, for passing this story down through the generations, in its various forms.

Appendix

The Library, by Apollodorus, cites that Lycaon "begat by many wives fifty sons." He then delivers the following list of names, unnumbered. When counted, the list only totals forty-nine.

Where is the name of the fiftieth son?

1. Melaeneus
2. Thesprotus
3. Helix
4. Nyctimus
5. Peucetius
6. Caucon
7. Mecisteus
8. Hopleus
9. Macareus
10. Macednus
11. Oenotrus
12. Polichus
13. Acontes
14. Euaemon
15. Ancyor
16. Archebates
17. Carteron
18. Aegaeon
19. Pallas
20. Eumon
21. Canethus
22. Prothous
23. Linus
24. Corethon
25. Maenalus
26. Teleboas
27. Physius
28. Phassus
29. Phthius
30. Lycius
31. Alipherus
32. Genetor
33. Bucolion
34. Socleus
35. Phineus
36. Eumetes
37. Harpaleus
38. Portheus
39. Plato(n)
40. Haemon
41. Cynaethus
42. Leo(n)
43. Harpalycus
44. Heraeeus
45. Titanas
46. Mantineus
47. Cleitor
48. Stymphalus
49. Orchomenus